Ladies, Ladies, Ladies
18 Vignettes

Kristen Zory King

*keep testing the spiny leaves
the spiny heart*
—Jane Hirshfield

© Kristen Zory King 2025
All rights reserved.
Published by Stanchion Books, LLC
StanchionZine.com
Edited by Katie Schmeling
Cover art by Jeff Bogle
Print ISBN: 979-8-89292-677-5

Table of Contents

Page 7 — The Last Friendly's in Cattaraugus County (Ladies)
Page 9 — Dead Ringer (Alice)
Page 13 — Controlled Burn (Talia)
Page 15 — And a Happy New Year (Laura-Jean)
Page 19 — Two Truths and a Lie (Callie)
Page 21 — Rutting Season (Vanya)
Page 23 — Neverland, New Mexico (Wendy)
Page 25 — Her Kingdom Come (Mother)
Page 27 — Miss Lonelyheart Herself (Audrey)
Page 31 — Executive Suite (Ladies)
Page 33 — Get It While You Can (Margot)
Page 37 — An Object in Motion (Elise)
Page 39 — Leaven, Rise (Marguerite)
Page 43 — The Cat Snatcher of Onondaga County (Mary)
Page 47 — A Fine Girl (Brandy)
Page 51 — Domestic Impression (Paige)
Page 53 — Hung the Moon (Girl Detective)
Page 57 — Wild Geese (Ladies)
Page 63 — Acknowledgements
Page 65 — About the Author

The Last Friendly's in Cattaraugus County (Ladies)

We never thought to ask her name but she loved us anyway, made sure we ate at least a spoonful of the ice cream she brought from the back, whipped cream and hot fudge melting into a lukewarm puddle at the bottom, gummy bears floating belly up. No charge for the extra scoop even though she knew we'd tip in change. Two of us weren't eating and the rest of us would soon follow, though only one ended up in rehab, a white walled place north of Pittsburgh. We traded tips we'd found on the internet—drink hot water to swell your stomach until it rounds, cut your food into tiny pieces and push it around the plate so your parents think you've eaten something, anything, enough, at least, not to be a worry—but saved the best ones for ourselves, disappearing into the pilled fleece of oversized sweatshirts, hoping one day, maybe, we'd vanish completely. But with the waitress we ate, sneaking bites of Black Raspberry or Hunka Chunka PB Fudge or the Monster Mash Sundae she would bring even though we were old enough to eat off the adult menu. If she was flirting with the grill cook we'd get broken waffle fries, onion rings charred dark and crispy in the fryer. *Honey,* she'd hum to any spoon left untouched, raising her eyebrows until each bowl was clear, even the sweet, tender meat of the cherry nose gone, and how hungry we were for this, for her, for the hope that, once emptied and clean we could allow ourselves to fill again. We even went to see her after prom, our eyes meeting across the damp, glittering room in agreement. Ditching our dates, our dresses whispered, ankles tangled together, as we climbed into the car, full in a way we hadn't been in years, of ourselves, of one another. But we were different girls by then, splintered by the futures sitting right in front of us, and as we reached the restaurant, the windows glowed empty, a sign on the front door saying *Thanks for 28 Years,* the waitress gone, as if we'd dreamed her.

Dead Ringer (Alice)

She couldn't quite make sense of it, but Alice was sure she saw herself standing on the corner of 17th and Ivy. It had been happening for a few days now: she'd be taking the dog for a walk, or standing in line at the bank, or driving to grab fresh basil, the one, crucial item that Ben had forgotten from the grocery store (honestly, why did she even bother with a list?), when her heart would stall in her chest, forgetting its steady rhythm as she saw herself standing just beyond. It wasn't a reflection, it was really her—her hair, cut in the way that framed her face and cost so much that she alternated credit cards each appointment, her shoulders, rolled back and down at the insistence of the personal trainer she saw four times each week, her expensive, retro-style clogs, the ones she'd bought at the outlet in Albany three years ago on one of those spring days that made her understand what the poet meant when she spoke of the thing with feathers, each bud around her standing sharp and primed to burst, seeking heat outside itself. Alice had once heard a voice on the radio say that women should buy clothing they found *aspirational,* remembered the girls from high school, nipples pert through soft, worn t-shirts, wooden heels peeking from flared jeans like a wink, and felt a brief moment of, well, not joy but maybe relief, as she paid the cashier in cash, the shoes swinging from a plastic bag on her wrist. In truth, she never wore them. They were heavy and made her ankles sore. They didn't match her black tights or silk blouses. But she liked to keep them at the front of her closet, liked the idea that one day, she would be the kind of woman who wore them. Perhaps that's what the radio had meant, that she should *aspire* to be weightless and free with the possibility of youth, that at any moment, she could skip second period, play hooky under the open blue sky, kiss a boy under the bleachers. That she could roll down the front windows in her car, feel it shake from the hum of her favorite song. That her hair could tangle with the smell of bonfire. That she could stop running her tongue over memories and hopes that lived in her mouth like a tooth grown sore and rotten with age. Leaning toward the windshield, Alice made to get a better look at the doppelganger in front of her, surprised herself as the slight weight of her chest prompted a timid honk from the horn in her steering wheel. With a start, Alice's foot left the brake and she rolled into the car ahead of her, not hard enough to hurt, just to raise the insurance premium. Ben would be furious, though at least it would give him something to do. As Alice exchanged numbers with the driver (*really, so sorry, just lost myself for a moment there*), she looked around for herself but found the street empty, not a trace remaining of the other woman with ripe flesh over soft bone, shoulders relaxed and hips balanced in high, timbered heels. Only the sun moving slowly against another afternoon.

Controlled Burn (Talia)

That night, Talia got so mad she traced a sharp line from bedroom to kitchen, removed a jar of salsa from the pantry and threw it straight down onto the ground, small, sticky drops of red staining the floor, the walls, the hidden corners behind the fridge. She considered, for a moment, dousing the mass of pulp and shard with what was left of the handle of vodka by the sink—a gift from her sister on her last birthday, the good stuff, given with instruction to drink only in celebration, good cheer—and set match to mess. But standing in front of the mosaic stained in front of her, Talia felt herself calm, the anger lit between her collarbones grown thin and weak, like smoke from a candle blown out with a wish. She took a deep breath in through her nose and released it with a hum from her throat. It was three years before she got mad enough to do it again.

And a Happy New Year (Laura-Jean)

As the postal box accepted her offering with a hard metal slap, Laura-Jean began to sweat. She had always considered herself a good person, kind, the type to deliver blushing bouquets of peonies to friends just because, write heartfelt notes in the corners of coworkers' birthday cards. She was not the kind of person to send vulgarities through the mail. Or, at least, she wasn't until suddenly, she was, the letter deep in the belly of the hollow box and the sky wary with December behind her.

It had seemed like a great idea, brave even, in her kitchen not yet twenty minutes ago, her tea losing steam as she addressed each envelope in small, cursive lettering. In just a few weeks, the calendar would turn toward a whole New Year, plump with promise. But Laura-Jean was not in the mood for a celebration, had never cared for the holiday which always seemed too fluorescent, too sticky. Was it an ending or a beginning? A look toward the future or the past? Laura-Jean was a woman comfortable with routine—the known trail through the grocery store (produce to dairy to cereal to snack), hair (straight and parted down the middle since first grade), the custard from her father's famous Boston Cream Pie (always eaten first, carved from in between thick slices of yellow cake, chocolate glaze). No, she was not looking forward to the midnight countdown, found herself nauseous at the thought. Nevertheless, she moved through her task, the pile of letters beside her growing larger as she worked to ignore the one name that had been crossed off the list.

She had always liked his mother, or rather, tried to be liked. And for six years, it had worked and they had been a kind of family, not intimate perhaps, but united by polite phone calls and soft longings. But all of that was gone now, because *apparently,* he was unhappy and *apparently,* Laura-Jean was the cause (the conversation surprising, sudden, and *apparently,* without room for debate). And so it was over, all of it: the long mornings in bed, bodies warm in defiance of the cool air of her apartment, the love notes hidden in pockets as she folded his worn jeans, the relationships with his family and friends tended to with such care, precision.

Except, it wasn't over, or so she'd reasoned. Relationships ended, sure, but the peripheral objects still remained: the animal smell of his flannel left on her couch, which she had yet to bring herself to clean; the song on the radio she couldn't hear without the echo of his whistle, off-key; the gentle memory of his mother's hand squeezing hers in approval, when talk turned to marriage, children. Perhaps that was why it was so painful. It was like when she had her tonsils removed, the abscess carved out of her throat but the lymph nodes still swollen and tender for weeks. Phantom pain—a hoary fog left behind. This was not the future she had been promised. As her stack thickened, she'd decided to add one final letter to the pile. *Wishing you a very merry! And a bright New Year!* But as she signed her name, she felt the swell of the wound and, on impulse, added five final words before sealing the letter and bracing the cold on the walk to the postbox. *P.S. Your son's a fucking asshole.*

And so Laura-Jean was sweating, the letter about to make its final goodbye from her kitchen counter to the processing center in Bethel, Pennsylvania, and then southbound toward the house where she once hoped to bring grandchildren. As she unzipped the heavy fleece of her jacket, allowing the cool winter air to rush her chest, Laura-Jean remembered what it felt like to be unburdened by her heart. And wasn't this what all the hullabaloo was about, anyway? What touching creatures, humans, always seeking a way to start again, despite known ritual, routine—new moon, new day, new week, new year. An ugly hope, or rather, brave, this faith that something better, something crisp and clean, just might be waiting in every ending, each new beginning. There was nothing to do now but walk home, put the kettle on to boil, prepare for work. Perhaps she'd call Alice or get takeout for dinner from the new Peruvian place down the street, the one she'd been wanting to try for ages. Suddenly, Laura-Jean had a good feeling about January, the month waiting for her, just ahead. And besides, she thought, he really was a dick.

Two Truths and a Lie (Callie)

Callie didn't have a tragedy of her own so she collected others, keeping them in her pocket and running her fingers against each scissored edge until they were so familiar by touch, so worn to the warmth of her fingertips, that she could almost believe they were hers. There were the obvious, daily ones, pulled out for sympathy at parties: the divorced parents or vague childhood trauma, the family dog run over in front of her very eyes, his insides pink as Pepto through clumped, matted fur. These were great for warm basements with half burned Christmas lights and shitty, cheap beer when hardly anyone was listening to her anyway. She didn't need to add much detail, the stories already familiar in their suburban haze. She saved the good ones for special occasions, for the teachers whose attention shifted, always, towards the pointed breasts and delicate wrists of girls in class, the boys who would make excuses to leave immediately after she blew them in her car, the heat from their bodies still smeared against the windows. When they would start checking their phones, the time, when the conversation returned over and over to the classes they shared together, to grades or weather or football, she'd sigh and pull one out, something like: *you remind me of my brother. He passed away a few years ago. He was at a party, drank too much. Our neighbor found him in her pool the next morning.* She liked to watch the words as they left her mouth, wormed their way into someone else's brain, liked the way the boys blinked hard, twice, the carefully saved secret taking them away, if only for a moment, from themselves. Made them feel a soft lick of fear on their necks, understand how scared they should be, of the world, of her, of this stupid fucking town, of never getting out. I don't remember the first lie she told me, the woe tinny and artificial, too pedestrian to stick, but I do remember the last one about best friends and forever and never being farther than a phone call. There were only two honest things about Callie: her loneliness and her blonde hair, which she wore long and, from the shine of it, had never been dyed. But I loved her anyway, slipping my tongue between her teeth even when she asked me not to, said our kisses weren't anything but practice, a way to pass the time.

Rutting Season (Vanya)

It's not that Vanya had a particular affection for deer, it's just that they were so obvious—all that sinew and muscle, the internal mechanics so similar to the men, from artery to liver to lungs, that it was a natural fit for their denaturing. The stomachs were tricky, the division always making a mess of her kitchen, but it was worth it for the horns: the white-eyed panic as bone pierced and threaded through skin, the sudden added weight to elongated neck, transmuted spine. On occasion, Vanya would be asked if her hands could be used to turn husband to pig, or perhaps something small enough to be picked up or kicked around. But her answer, always, was simple: a deer knew its place in the family order. Deer could be led, did not walk head first into danger, at least, not knowingly. And should they refuse the lesson, believe the copper taste beneath their tongues to be anything but a warning, well, first frost was coming and the village hunters liked rutting season best.

Neverland, New Mexico (Wendy)

The only time Wendy reads her horoscope is when she is stoned, but as she has been stoned for the better part of three years now, she understands her heart more as celestial being than animal object. It started out as a way to help her sleep, one restless night turning into a dozen and then a dozen more and soon she was ready to try anything and, remembering the sweet burn of her teenage years (the years after, of course, when she understood in totality the depth of her decision, that she could never go back, never, never), found a boy down the street to sell her an eighth, his small nose pert and eyes darting in a way that felt familiar, the flower harsh and dry but good enough to help her brain slow mercifully as her body wove into the quilt beneath her. A cancer cusp, Wendy is never more than one bad day away from leaving it all behind. And why not? Try as she might, she can never quite find her way back to the one place she knows as home, though the route maps hot through her veins. What would be so bad about a clean slate? America, maybe. New Mexico, with its desert sky and high noon. Wendy reads her Sun sign first, and then her Rising, ending with Moon and occasionally Venus, seeking and seeking until she finds what she is looking for: a compass reaching right on toward morning, a calm for this itch, shallow as a scab. Better yet are the signs, good omens—an orange peel withered on the sidewalk when she's only just dreamed of eating clementines with her mother; her brothers' names written in the corner of a library book; the fairylike tinkle of a wind chime on a walk around town—each a small sliver of starlight, a humble invitation to begin again. Right now, they say. You don't need to stay sewn to your shadow. Fight hook and crook for this life of yours. Don't ever beg for mercy. Assume, always, that dawn will arrive and with it, mischief, mermaid song, magic. Isn't all you need faith, trust, a pinch of pixie dust? At night, frost sits at Wendy's window, cracked slightly to let out the smoke and stale air from her lungs. Squinting toward the horizon, she allows red rocks to rush her vision. Mist off distant mountain. Cacti with virgin bloom.

Her Kingdom Come (Mother)

There was a funny turn to Mother's mouth when she saw the ants each summer, a tightness to the lips so that they were colored only by a faint over-layer of the paling pink tint she put on in the mornings. It was a color both too young and too old for her, evoking the light, pollen-like powder puffs of a more glamorous and long-gone era and the uncertainty of a teenager who's just agreed to a ride home from the school quarterback. There were traces of it everywhere: a blur of pink on the rim of her milky coffee cup, the butts of half-ashed cigarettes. She even kissed closed the little notes she'd send along in our lunch boxes, a reminder of both her love and her reach. Every July she'd stand at the window and watch as the ants made a steady and solid trail over the sink and toward any crumb my brother or father or I left lingering, her eyes narrowed, her fingers holding a single bleeding ice cube to the soft pulse on her neck. She was quick with immediate attacks—white domed traps in every corner, bottles of Windex which flattened their small bodies on impact and left a chemical taste to the air— but her favorite, the most unforgiving, was boiled water. Circling the perimeter of the house, she'd calmly watch for any small movement, cracks in the sidewalk, a glowing blush from the sun on the back of her neck. And then she'd return to the kitchen, shoulder blades arched and pointed through the back of her summer linen, and place a large pot of water to boil on the stove. Once it hissed, she'd return to the spot, handling the prize from the kitchen with yellow gloved hands and pouring the scalding liquid directly onto the shivering mass. *Only way to kill the queen*, she'd say, giving no consideration to the small burns rising on her skin in the naked space between her dress and house shoes. Task complete, she'd return to the house, taking her place by the window to watch over her kingdom, something gleeful and dangerous sitting patient in the small corners of her lips.

Miss Lonelyheart Herself (Audrey)

Audrey leaves the door to the bathroom open when she showers, an invitation rarely answered by the strangers in her bed. It's not that she's particularly interested in sex, more that she finds herself both taut and tangled by love as if caught helpless in the pull of a hurricane, the air around her warm and lightly green with the hint of total devastation. What she wants is to be eaten alive, swallowed whole in one round, full bite. She wants to listen to Elvis as if what he sings is true. Wants to watch goosebumps rise on her arms as she moves away from the water above, allowing another body to slip beside hers. Wants a constellation of hickeys purpling her collarbone, a stray streak of soap gently washed from her back by another's hand, someone to think about at the dentist.

Most often she returns to her bedroom, skin humid and freshly flushed, to find it empty. She'll allow herself a small moment to notice that the bed has been made, albeit in haste, a kind of apology which must count for something. No matter. Just this week Audrey has fallen in love twelve times at least, a full baker's dozen if you count the way her heart stood quiet and still in her chest as she walked past the park where a young father picked puffed dandelions for his child, holding each stem close to sticky cheek, fat, wet mouth. There was also the bartender on the corner, delicate reminders of *Call Nina / Cat Food* inked on his thick forearm. There was her neighbor, the graduate student, who knocked gently, so gently, before sliding the mail misdelivered to his apartment under her door. There was the woman on the bus, a thumb print fogging the left lens of her glasses. Even the author on the back of Audrey's book jacket, who looked at her with such clever eyes she found herself winking in return. In a flash, Audrey is mother, wife, Nina, lover, stranger, and oh, how sweet to open her mouth and drink straight from this faucet, the slanted purity of maybe, of almost, of one day, sliding fast and deep down her throat.

Once, when Audrey was seventeen, she woke to the sound of her two best friends outside her window. It was August, weeks before the start of senior year, the future bloated and bright in front of them. Ian's mother had a list of approved college applications, all private and pre-med. Audrey hoped to go West, write movies. And Callie didn't care where she was going or why, so long as she never saw this place again. Quick and quiet, Audrey pulled on her shorts to join them, the three pedaling through streets dark and known. After a few aimless minutes, Ian suggested the tennis court and they made their way over, dropping their bikes in the dry grass to lie side by side and watch the sky. As Audrey listened to her friends settle into a debate of airplane or shooting star, she felt the ruinous burst of something gorgeous behind her chest. She'd had a wink of this feeling before, usually when Callie showed up to homeroom seconds before the bell, her hair still damp and curled from the shower. But tonight it was bigger, grand and gilded and honeyed with the last of summer. If someone were to hold a dandelion close to her own mouth, if she were to close her eyes to wish and blow, she'd wish for the same thing she'd wished for since that night: a crisp moon, a bruise on her left knee, the heat rising from the sun-stained turf through to her pelvis.

What could be more noble than this: the naked extension of oneself toward another? Audrey runs the shower hot, fogging up the small room and leaving a faint vapor scented with lavender on the wood frame of the bathroom door. Eyes closed, she gives in to a brief slip of hope that a body will slide into the steam behind her to press flesh wet and slick and hard against her back. It fills her, this feeling, the humid air a storm alive around her. When asked if she's ever felt her heart break, she has two answers: *Every single second of every single day.* And: *Yes, once.* Audrey draws her name in the condensation on the shower wall, traces a heart big and sloppy around it, hums *love me tender, love me sweet,* erases it all with the meat of her palm.

Executive Suite (Ladies)

We once had a boss who kept his office door open. We once had a boss who took in strays. We once had a boss who sipped orange juice from a carton, repeated *good morning, ladies* once, twice, three times a piece. We once had a boss with hair wrapped tight around his knuckles. We once had a boss with cholesterol a mile high. We once had a boss who brought tuna for lunch—the first half gone by 10:45, the second disappearing just before close.

We once had a boss who put hot sauce in his coffee. We once had a boss who never learned how to sing. We once had a boss who hated loose change, shook it loose like dice in his palms before handing to us for keeps. We once had a boss who measured his hands across our shoulders. We once had a boss who we made *so proud*. We once had a boss who played footsie under the table, our tights worn and running round the calves from each shadowed *tap tap tap*.

We once had a boss who drove us home. We once had a boss who really liked it when we wore that sweater. We once had a boss with a mistress (*shhhhh*). We once had a boss with a wife (*don't look at me like that*). We once had a boss with a daughter (*you *remind me so much of her*). We once had a boss with three (*enough to make a man drink*).

We once had a boss who never laughed. We once had a boss who whistled through his nose. We once had a boss who went on vacation to Boca Raton. We once had a boss who never returned. We once had a boss who yelled so loud, spit flew into his own eye. We once had a boss who lied about his birthday. We once had a boss with sweat stains dyed dark into the fabric beneath each arm.

We once had a boss who smelled like cat. We once had a boss who smelled like fish. We once had a boss who smelled of penny, cheap cologne, hotel soap, sweat, orange juice, vinegar, coffee, fear, promise, wool, detergent, pain. We once had a boss who kept his hands in his pockets. We once had a boss with a retainer and a lisp. We once had a boss who—*don't be so sensitive, ladies*—kept his office door closed.

Get It While You Can (Margot)

When Margot was a child, she would wait until no one was looking and dip a small strand of her hair into her ice cream. Not the whole strand, just the tip, a half inch or so, enough to coat and harden slightly, leaving a little taste for later. She was patient with this treat, keeping it carefully tucked behind her ear until she needed it most, the weight of the strand soothing, known. Sometimes that was before bed: placing the strand gently on her tongue, she'd allow the sticky clump to soften slowly as she fell asleep and left her hot, cramped bedroom behind. Often, she waited until school the next day. She could always tell when Ms. Peters was in a real mood and would save the gift until the last second, sinking into the sugared grit of hair and cream at recess or during a quiz on fractions. It was a small and singular joy, something she knew to keep to herself lest her father find out, call her *greedy little porker*. Her mother would probably go for the scissors. Margot knew that happiness was hard to come by. Sometimes you just had to make it yourself.

So sorry, Margot texted her boss, a man 14 years her junior. She was half an hour late for the meeting. *Looks like he's going to need emergency surgery. Taking the rest of the day but I'll make sure you have the quarterly report by Friday.* Margot was not, in fact, seeing to the needs of her ancient dachshund, already old by the time he was rescued and gone blind and deaf with age. She did not even have a dog, much less one that required diapers, though the amount of recent emergencies her pet had undergone in the last few months would probably mean she would need to have a dog funeral sometime soon. What she did have was a banana split and a free afternoon. She wondered if the death of a pet would qualify for a few extra hours off, on account of the bereavement and all.

She had fantasized about the banana split for days, imagining the thick, creamy puddles each flavor would make as they melted together, the hot fudge, heavy on top of each sugary mound. Just the thought of a plump red cherry, whipped cream, each tender chopped nut between her molars was enough to get her through the moments between morning shower— her body bruised crimson beneath the scalding water —and bed. She'd held off since Monday, finding something edged and shadowed and holy in this abstinence, anticipation, but she'd known today was the day when she'd woken up to find Todd gone, again. He was on an exercise kick, rising an hour and a half earlier than her to head to the gym and *get in a good sweat* but for whose benefit, she wasn't yet sure.

Likely Elise, office temp turned secretary, but the cliche of it was too precious for Margot to consider.

The ice cream shop was cold and outside, snow fell in a quiet, dangerous way. Margot imagined that they did not get many customers in February, cut corners by turning down the heat and offering a limited selection of toppings. The walls, sun-faded and pastel yellow, did nothing to cheer up the place. Glancing around the shop Margot was surprised to find that she was alone, the teenager at the counter likely in the back cleaning or getting high. She watched the snow erase each harsh line of the street beyond, covering the sidewalk, her car, the hand carved sign for the shop. Taking a small strand of her hair, she dipped it lovingly into the mess of chocolate and strawberry, canned pineapple. *Fuck it,* she thought, lifting the tip directly to her lips. *Get it while you can.*

An Object in Motion (Elise)

Three fingers deep inside her and back against the wall, Elise wonders at the way in which she always seems to find herself in this position. Using the crook of her knee, she pulls the man closer to her, puts his mouth to her neck and looks toward the stuccoed ceiling so as not to acknowledge the shine from the bare skin circling his crown, the sweat pooling into the deep crease between his head and neck. She knows that if she guides them—the men—they will lose themselves in their concentration, immediate disciples to her lead, and she, in turn, can relax and just think, allow her eyes to blur into the deep mauve of the mid-range hotel curtains. There were more meaningful ways to ruminate, of course, but none so quick as this particular pleasure, occasional pain. Just this morning, Elise found another letter in her mailbox. The return address in the corner was hopeful, bordered with three hearts and a star, the lettering large and carefully done, though the "s" in her name was backwards, reminding her of a garden snake. This wasn't a part of the agreement. Placing the letter back in the box, Elise had found her shoes and prepared quickly for a run, but three miles in she knew it wasn't enough. She needed a way to sink deeper into herself. Elise had once visited a shaman down south who said that hers was a body in motion, something she'd already understood about herself, though she was glad a higher power seemed to agree. She was most comfortable when moving, swaying her body lightly through meetings, fingers across keyboards, tapping the heel of her foot against restaurant floor or hard shin, pushing her pelvis toward palm. She didn't even mind the occasional sob nor vomit—the violent thrust of her body being emptied. It was generous, this movement, a meditation or gift to herself, a warm breath in, a sour breath out. The man removes his fingers and, grinning, licks them one by one. Elise resists the urge to roll her eyes, and kicks him toward the bed, enjoying, for a moment, the flexed look of her calf. Are her daughter's legs also strong? Is hers, too, a body designed to lose itself in motion: a run through recess, a furious twirl? Clearing her throat, Elise spits phlegm hot and thick straight onto the man's chest, returns to the ceiling, the curtains, herself.

Leaven, Rise (Marguerite)

Before she disappeared, Marguerite decided she would learn to make bread. She thought about this as she walked along the rocky beach one autumn morning, considering just how to do it.

"Do it," was how Marguerite thought of her forthcoming exit, a vanishing act hopefully brief and slightly distasteful, not meriting too much description. She would likely do it in January. She didn't want to make a fuss with the holidays coming up and besides, everyone was sad in January so she imagined people would be a little more understanding than they usually were in these kinds of situations. But first, yes, before the careful, quiet packing, the transition into a morning cold and clear, she would learn the simple art of flour, water, yeast.

She wasn't sure what, exactly, it was about her walk along the shore that prompted this new desire, a deviation from her usual melancholic musings. Perhaps it was the salt in the air, reminding her of childhood summers spent on a beach just like this, all sharp edges and coarse sand. Mother would leave the dough to rise all night and then wake up early to place it in the oven, the pungent smell of yeast rising through the old house, water-beaten and gray. And then the children, too, would rise, as if summoned, to sit around the breakfast table, wiping the crust from their eyes as they laughed, trading dreams and dropping fat dollops of local preserve onto the bread, fresh from the oven. Oh, how Marguerite loved those mornings, wanted to wrap their sleepy warmth around her.

Or perhaps it was because, in the same way these walks gave purpose to her lungs, her legs, baking bread would give her a use for her hands. Marguerite had never really known what to do with her hands, so mostly they hung useless at her side. It drove her husband crazy. *For God's sake*, he'd say, grabbing her wrists and placing them on his leg, the small of his back. *Don't just lie there, Marguerite. Touch me.*

She could probably use her hands to write letters, but she could rarely think of anyone to write to. And she'd always wanted to paint, sew, perhaps even garden, but knew she'd be useless. Recently, Joana, from the coffee shop in town, had invited Marguerite to a drawing class, apples and pears placed in bowls and traced lightly in charcoal. Nervously, Marguerite had agreed—the class was on a Wednesday, a night her husband worked late. Marguerite had often imagined spending time with Joana outside of the small cafe, an image that caught tight in her throat. But as they pulled up to the studio, she found herself quickly overwhelmed by the scent of the woman beside her, a faint smell of flower, soap, that Marguerite had wanted, with blushing urgency, to taste. Feigning migraine, Marguerite left the class early, rolling the windows down and removing her gloves on the drive home, her fingers chapping red and raw from October's crisp chill.

Walking along the beach, waves frothing beside her, Marguerite allowed her mind to float freely—toward memory, reverie, plan for escape—telling her husband later *and just like that, I was back in the parking lot, half a mile away. It was like I was asleep. It was like I had just woken up.* It was often like this. She walked seven miles every morning, beginning just off the parking lot near the north entrance, down to the fallen hickory, sea soaked and covered in lichen, and turning back around, all the while stopping here and there to take a long, deep breath. This area of the beach smelled mostly like dead things, but she didn't mind. Everything died sooner or later, the smells left behind no longer their business.

And then she would keep walking and stop again to breathe in and out and then walk and stop again and between all of this walking and stopping and inhaling and exhaling she would think and think and think. Oh, how wonderful that sticky orange preserve, the way the smell would stay on her fingers. (The sweet sound of Joana's laugh.) (How long before Marguerite's husband noticed she was gone?) Oh, how horrible it was when she made Henry so mad he walked upstairs, grabbed her journal and threw it right into the ocean. (The small mark on Joana's neck, peach, pink, no larger than a penny.) (Should she pack three sweaters or two?) Oh, how kind it was of Daddy to bring them to the beach, even after Mother died, though she knew he didn't like to do anything that summer, except smoke in his room. (Joana's fingernails, clipped short and clean). (How long would the small slip of cash, tucked neatly behind the bread box, truly last?)

Marguerite imagined the way the dough would feel in her hands, elastic and heavy and resistant. She imagined digging her palms into the sticky mixture, pounding her fist hard to remove any lump. She imagined a streak of flour across her cheek, painting its twin on the soft cheek of another. Nearing the end of her trail, Marguerite surprised herself as she turned toward the path into town. What could it hurt to pick up some yeast? Perhaps stop by the coffee shop for a quick cup of peppermint tea? She felt, for a moment, the relief in rising. Perhaps tomorrow she would give it a try.

The Cat Snatcher of Onondaga County (Mary)

In the moments before Mary became the Cat Snatcher of Onondaga County, she was struck with a sudden vision of happiness. It was an evening alive with the promise of summer, May in violent bloom around her and the air both warm and slightly damp with the smell of iris. In many ways, the night was like any other: Mary's shadow slight against the fading light as she walked alone on the short loop she never missed, come spring snowstorm or paling summer. But on this evening, Mary, a little buzzed from the loosely rolled joint hidden in her palm, locked eyes with the most beautiful tabby she'd ever seen. The cat, an aloof gentleman with coarse, matted fur, was crossing the street ahead of her when he stopped, held strong to her gaze as she walked gently toward him hoping he wouldn't spook and run off. But he wasn't afraid, his body still and then swaying toward hers. He even let Mary pet him, folding his head back into her stroking hand to make sure she got between his ears. It was thrilling to be needed in such a specific, simple way.

When Mary thought back to that evening, she remembered first the calm that set in her chest, hands against the small, warm body and the future unfurling in front of her like a fiddlehead stretching toward final form. She remembered the tabby, skin loose around his bones, as well as all the other cats she'd seen on her loop around town, both the strays outside and those sitting regal in the windows of the houses she'd passed, the setting sun on their bellies, their roost, ruled. Mary had always been a bit of an indoor cat herself. She was terrible at parties, uncomfortable away from her home, worn and warm, familiar, never knowing quite what to say and inching, always, toward the corner, a can of soda slowly losing its fizz from the warmth in her palms. She remembered, yes, a shift, her shoulders scrunching toward her ears as she considered the tabby and all those left to roam, fend for themselves while their owners enjoyed pinot on the porch or put the children to bed without a thought given to thorn stuck in soft paw, the car stopped two seconds too late, the small and noble being they had promised, in the fickle way of all promises, to love and care for, despite odd scratch or hairball vomit.

She remembered—soft fur nuzzled against her knuckles—how obvious it had seemed. An act of kindness, really. An answer, invitation, offering, a divine ministry: take the tabby home. Set him up with his own seat by the window where he could never be hurt, where she could always take care of him. What she saw in her vision that evening wasn't love, but something cousin to conscious, calling. She saw a house, her house, still quiet but full of the warm hum of life, of little paws, of soft purrs. She saw first, the tabby, but then another, and then another—the street was truly full of them, would their negligent owners even notice?—until before her was a little family of sorts, always growing, always happy. She could start with the tabby, tucked against her chest. Next, a small black thing, thin and sleek, the bell around her neck singing gently as she was ushered into the passenger seat. As summer dawned, so too could her menagerie. Another tabby (backyard). Calico (porch). Siamese (tricky). Three-legged fluff. Shortened tail. One well fed. Another half feral. Oh, the chorus of toes clicking against tile. The happiness a psalm whistled from her throat through to her nose.

What Mary didn't see in her vision that evening were the posters: some printed on blue ink that ran in the rain, others drawn with crayon, all begging for information on their lost little one. She didn't see the travel of whispers that started as a joke, but grew prickly, dangerous, in grocery aisle and line behind post office counter as the summer wore on and her small family grew. She didn't see the headlines in the local paper detailing the sudden disappearance of the cats around town, the police chief's personal line written in red at the bottom. Didn't hear the shatter of rock against window, the sharp knock on her front door from a group of local men, didn't anticipate the hard beat of her heart as she stood still and quiet in her bedroom, waiting for them to leave.

No, in this moment, it was still seconds before and Mary was not yet the Cat Snatcher of Onondaga County, did not see the dark morning she would drive her van around town just before sunrise, opening the door one by one as she returned each cat to his first family. On this evening, summer all around her, Mary was just a regular woman, palms open to the promise of happiness right in front of her.

A Fine Girl (Brandy)

Sandy is just getting to the good part of his story, his voice a quick and high tenor, when I hold up my hand signaling the need for a break. I can tell by the way the shadows are moving that the sun will set soon, and I can't miss it. Won't. I refill Sandy's glass and grab my sweater, the promise of a long winter already sharp in the air though it's only just September. The sunsets are getting longer too, the reds staining that part of the sky where it meets the ocean for whole minutes after the sun has disappeared.

When I return, Sandy is smiling that mean smile of his, eyes half closed and a hard wheeze in his throat. I haven't been gone more than eight minutes but he's not happy to have been interrupted, got the first lick of a buzz on him and decided to be cruel with it. *Remember that fella'd blow in here each summer? Some kind of sailor-boy, wasn't he?* Yes, yes, I remember, Sandy knows that. But I won't give him the satisfaction. *Lotta men blow in here come April or August, Sandy*, I say as I turn my attention to dusting the second shelf of the bar, the last of the day's light illuminating each small particle, like tiny, bright wishes caught in the air. The bell rings over the door and Sam enters, earlier than normal, but then again it's Tuesday, a day with its own particular flavor of sorrow.

Sam heads straight to the jukebox and I grab a cheap merlot from the back for when he's ready to join us. *Another round, Sandy?* I can't help but soften. Of course Sandy's curious, they all were. Still are, especially on nights I wear the locket, it's shine hard against the hollowed dip in my throat. But that's old news now and the Sailor hasn't been to this port for years. The fourth season was the hardest. The first, I made a fool of myself, getting dressed up each night and leaving the bar lights on an hour past close, despite the teasing. The second I knew not to get my hopes up, but hope is funny that way, always clawing behind your breastbone like a kitten, and I'd be lying if I said I didn't wear a little mascara each night just in case. I don't remember much about the third except the sex. I was so angry, I'd fuck just about any seafaring man that walked through my door, half hoping the Sailor'd come by and catch me on my knees. But the fourth was when I understood he was gone. Whether he'd died, or quit, or found another woman, I don't know and who was there to ask? Besides, he'd made no promise to me. For some men, home is an ever-moving coastline.

I'm not stupid. I know there were as many women as there were harbors and that a man like that needs the fantasy of a wife waiting and wanting, on days the water winks with the promise of a good, long sleep. Sometimes I like to imagine us all together, the Sailor's women, the stories we could tell. I'd close the bar early, grab some cheese from that sweet little shop in Portland, have them all over to my apartment with its kitchenside view of the sea. I can hear the way we'd laugh—not the kind that women use with company, a quick, polite cough, but the real kind, a deep, delicious bellyful. It would be strange at first, all of us sizing up the other, wondering who was better in bed, comparing the bloat of our stomachs, the fullness of our breasts, but women like us know we'll never sing louder than the sea, and we'd get over it quickly. Besides, our time with the Sailor was not the kind of thing you're meant to question, just grab on to for as long as the grip will hold. I know it sounds ridiculous. It was ridiculous. But the Sailor gave us, gave me, something more than love, silver chains and the soft promise of summer.

I could always tell when he'd left the bed, the cool absence of his body rousing me from even the deepest of sleep. The first time I woke without him beside me I'd cried, ashamed at the idea of having been left in the night, ashamed more at myself for caring. We were new to each other then, all warm hands between warmer thighs, and I could hardly get enough of him, would have licked him clean if he'd have let me. But he'd returned to bed in short order, smelling clean and sharp like the fog off the dawning sea. *Where do you go in the mornings?* I'd finally asked, after the fourth or fifth time. He was quiet so long I made to drop it, until I noticed the shine in his eyes. His voice low, he told me of the water and not in the way that made the boys in the bar laugh. Told me his father and his father before that had promised to never take a day back on land for granted, watched the sun rise each morning and the sun set each night in thanks. It had the symmetry of a prayer and the next morning I joined him out back, watched as the sun kissed the sky until it blushed, a ritual that's stayed with me since, morning and night, no matter the season. His parting gift, I suppose.

Sam's joined us at the bar and the first notes of his favorite song make the air feel full and round. I don't know why he plays the same tune each night but it's not for me to ask, so I pour his drink and hum along. Sandy's returned to his story, the kind that stinks of salt water and shanties and Sam winks at me as I fill his glass to the rim. The sun is gone now, the bar only half lit on account of that one burned out bulb I can never quite reach. I listen to Sandy's story, fill up my own glass from Sam's bottle, and think about what it means to love a stranger, what a good wife I could have been, give thanks for the sunrise that's sure to come tomorrow.

Domestic Impression (Paige)

At the museum, Paige stops in front of a painting of a woman sitting in a chair, her shoulders exhausted, head heavy and balanced in her hands. Stepping closer, Paige notices a slight tilt to the woman's head, as though she is listening to someone just beyond. It is a domestic scene, the card on the right reads, impressionist. Paige considers this word, "domestic," wonders if the curator was referring to the kitchen seeped in thick and dusty hues of navy and charcoal or the sharp edges of despair jagged against each mellowed stroke of the painter's brush. She returns the next afternoon on her lunch break, stands again in front of the faceless figure, the room around both women still and silent. It is the first time in weeks that Paige has not felt alone. That night, she calls her sister again to try to explain, but is met by an automated recording stating that Talia's voice mailbox is full and no message can be received. Scraping leftover hamburger meat from her plate, she summons to mind the woman in the painting, imagines telling her the small details of the day. How nice to have someone to sit with, talk to. Someone who understands what it's like to wake up one morning and realize your life is halfway over and there are cobwebs in the kitchen corner. A sister who notices the winter light bleeding through the window. Turns her head to listen. Forgives.

Hung the Moon (Girl Detective)

The simple fact was this: the Girl Detective, no longer a detective nor, for more years than she cared to admit, a girl, was dying. She had imagined the moment often enough (death a constant suitor in her line of work), but she had always assumed her demise would come at the hands of villain or long-standing foe, not from her own body, eating away at itself in a desperate and failing attempt to get rid of malignant cells of unknown origin, multiplying at rapid speed. As she stared at the mouth of the doctor, his tongue periodically licking his top lip (nervous tick), she wished she could remember more of it all. There were moments, of course, the parlors smokey and still as she revealed the true killer; a glint of light off the plastered jewels of a false heiress; the way a collage of clues would rearrange themselves in her mind as she lay alone in bed in the early hours of the morning. But the adrenaline of her trade had made the details fade into something hazy and dim, each case a blur of facts she'd pieced together later from her own quotes in the newspaper.

Years ago, the Girl Detective had gotten into the habit of going to the movies when she was stuck on a case. She'd often choose a matinee, the theater mostly empty in the afternoon, allowing her to thrill at the darkness mossy around her, the quick bright flashes of light from the screen illuminating each bare seat like a gap-toothed smile. Sometimes she would even enjoy a cigarette and popcorn wet with butter as she sat back to watch colors drum against the screen, the puzzle's hum an echo throughout the open space of her skull.

Once, after a particularly trying afternoon, the film (romantic, dangerous) having done nothing to unlock the hidden question in her mind, she left the theater to find an early moon hanging bright above the parking lot, its belly round and slightly pink, the beauty of it making her feel, at once, alone and alive. It was during this time that, if she could avoid it, the Girl Detective had stopped leaving the house after dark—evenings assigned groups and pairs and things like going out to dinner (a lone glass of merlot, a book left cracked and open as she slipped toward the toilet, a meal delivered quickly to her party of one) made her spine curve with an ineffable sadness.

The Girl Detective had always considered her relationship with the moon to be largely cordial, one of mutual (if distant) respect. This was true of most of her relationships, her trade not leaving much time for phone calls nor pleasantries. When was the last time

she had heard from Bess? How old were George's twin
. . . boys? Girls? The Girl Detective had chosen a
different life, a life with limited space for shared
dessert, summer barbeques, hummus wiped lovingly
from the corner of her lip. And so, for some time, the
Girl Detective spent her afternoons at the cinema,
evenings alone at home. But that didn't stop the moon
from its call, its Tom-like Peep through the window.
The Girl Detective knew the moon would never know
her name (not even her father seemed to remember
anymore, so much was she Girl, so much was she
Detective), but in the same way it knew how to pull
the tide or quicken the pulse, it knew when she
needed the wink of a friend. And here it was, staring
boldly, waiting for her to leave the concrete building,
catch its eye. Heading back into the theater, the Girl
Detective (glowing, generous) gestured to the
teenager alone behind the counter. *Come here*, she
said, *I have something wonderful to show you.*

How odd to remember this now in the doctor's small,
private office, the back of her shoulders bare against
the chilled air. Not the countless victories, the golden
tipped luck of being right so many times in a row, the
brief, round taste of fame. Learning of her death
(progressing quickly) (the doctor's pink tongue) (it's
quick dart from behind his gums), she thought not of
the letters from her fan club, the men who poisoned

their wives thinking they could get away with it, the way the chief of police has ground his small little teeth when forced to present her with a medal of honor from the city. No, she remembered the boy who had joined her in the parking lot that night, catching his breath and smiling as he stared up at the moon, clean, ancient, known. For the first time in her life, the Girl Detective did not have a solution to the problem staring her in the face. But she had the quiet of an empty theater one afternoon in November, a moment shared in a parking lot, a life fully waxed, and now, at long last, ready to wane.

Wild Geese (Ladies)

It is early days: the weeks in which we are asked to stay indoors, the weeks in which we are wary of our neighbors, the weeks in which we ration squares of toilet paper, scrub our vegetables raw, bake bananas into bread, consider, for the first time in a long time, a whispered prayer. It is early days and each moment seems simultaneously shocking, sudden, searing, slow. We are asked not to touch one another. We hold our breath, despite the chilly spring air. Even those lucky enough to be together can smell something lonely, metallic, on each other's breath.

I am alone. I am in bed. I have been here since morning. There is a dull ache in my low back, a small rash on my thigh from the heat of my laptop. Books sit in piles around me, but I cannot focus on the words within. My belly is full and my fridge is empty from an anxious, numbing purge. I am caught helpless between two desires: to run, fast and wild until sweat maps from forehead to ankle, and to lie still, a childlike instinct to play dead.

My phone rings with an unknown number. I answer.

The voice on the other end of the line is thin. I imagine it attached to thin braids, to thin, translucent wrists, to a dress, thin and well worn, perhaps with small flowers embroidered at the collar. *Hello,* it starts before falling quiet. *Hi,* I respond, waiting.

Do you . . . do you have a moment? I'd like to share something with you. A scripture spills through the speaker at rapid speed. She is nervous but steadies the longer she reads. Alma. Nephi. Mosiah. I do not stop her, despite an initial flush of anger. But where do I have to be but here? Who do I have to be but witness? Besides, of course there will be proselytizing at the end of the world. We can't help ourselves. We want, so badly, to speak. We want, so badly, to believe. We want, so badly, to hold another's hand as we bear a world this bright, this brutal.

When she finishes, I hear her exhale quick and sharp, thrilled with her own bravery and grateful, I'd like to think, that there is a living, breathing thing still waiting at the other end of the line. But she falters. What to do now? It's unusual enough to have someone answer the call, let alone wade patient through each word. From the silence I am surprised to hear my own voice. *Thank you for sharing. May I share something with you?* Cautious, she agrees, and

I speak from memory, a poem I housed in my body years ago. *"You do not have to be good."*

When I am finished, she thanks me and we are shy as we consider this unexpected fellowship. She asks if she can call me again next week, share another scripture. I agree, though wariness still nips my ears. *Hey wait, what's your name?* I ask, just before I push the small red button on my phone that will bring me back to the quiet of my apartment. *Ada,* she replies. *Kate,* I answer.

We continue this way the following week and then the next, her voice full of verse, mine of memory and lyric. *This poem is from my college professor,* I say. *I read this scripture when I'm angry,* she responds. *Here's Whitman,* I offer. *Oliver. Clifton. Rumi. Gay.* Sometimes she sings, and the sound charms me. *What made you smile today?* I ask. *Fresh butter with dinner. That the snow has almost melted and the fields are fresh with mud. Wool socks.* Neither of us name the phone call, though I know we've both waited, watched the clock move slowly from one afternoon to the next.

I tell her secrets, but not the big ones. Ones like: *There's almost nothing I love more than a store-bought pastry. The kind with sweet, cheap jam in the middle, frosting, dough dry enough to leave a trail of crumbs from your thumb to the corners of your lip. The kind that brings ants if you let them. I could eat a whole box on my own. They remind me of vacation. Ocean City. Myrtle Beach. Something my mom bought to keep my cousins quiet.* In return she tells me her own but they are shadowed, the kind of things you can only tell a stranger in the dark hum of your own room, and they are not mine to share.

On our fourth call together there is an edge behind her voice. I try to find our rhythm but it is slippery and unknown. I ask if I can share a poem and she does not respond. *So, are you going to accept Jesus Christ as the source of truth and redemption, light and life, or not?* I can tell she's unfamiliar with this fury but likes the sting of it as it leaves her throat. *No, Ada* I reply, though I know it will mark the end of this barter, so tender, so true. *Then I can't call you anymore, Kate,* she says, too loud, and I remember an old friend who once told me that anger is the quickest way for grief to leave the body.

I do not know how to say goodbye to this girl, woman, neither stranger nor, really, friend. She does not know how to say goodbye to me, and the silence between us stuns before I hear her, finally, hang up. The sun has grown longer since her first call and my apartment is just now growing dim. I open the door to wave in the air of early evening, warmer now. Fresh. I boil water for tea. I wonder if the calf she helped nurse to health is continuing to thrive. I wash my hands, for good measure. *"Meanwhile, the world goes on."*

Acknowledgements

A creative work of any kind takes, among other things, an extraordinary amount of patience—from the artist, yes, but frankly, most often, from all those they are lucky enough to hold dear. With this in mind, my deep gratitude to the many people whose kindness and patience helped bring this little chapbook to life.

To Katie Schmeling, for her generous editing and to Jeff Bogle, for his unwavering belief in and publication of my work, as well as the work of so many emerging writers.

To Kathy Fish, Sara Lippmann, and David Byron Queen, in whose workshops many of these stories were first imagined, as well as to the many workshop peers and literary community, in Washington, DC and beyond, who helped make each draft stronger, both during the workshop container as well as long after (here's looking at you, Philip!).

To the various residencies and fellowships that allowed me the time, space, and support needed to both explore these stories and find creative rest, including, but not limited to: the DC Commission on the Arts and Humanities Fellowship, the Nancy Ludmerer Fellowship for Flash Fiction and corresponding residency at The Porches Writing

Retreat in Norwood, Virginia, the Chulitna Arts Residency in Lake Clark, Alaska, and the Sable Arts Residency in Stockbridge, Vermont.

To the following publications, within which earlier versions of these stories found their first home:

Twin Pies Literary—Rutting Season (December 2020)
Tiny Molecules—The Last Friendly's in Cattaraugus County (March 2021)
The Citron Review—Her Kingdom Come (June 2021)
    Selected for the "Best Microfiction 2022"
    Anthropology by Tania Hershman
The Jarnal: Volume II—Dead Ringer (August 2022)
The Jarnal: Volume II—Two Truths and a Lie (August 2022)
Stanchion—A Fine Girl (August 2022)
Stanchion—Miss Lonelyheart Herself (October 2023)

And finally, to my family, friends, students, teachers, neighbors, and *darling, darling, darling ladies* for your varied offerings of support—from hand holding to paddleboarding, long walks in Rock Creek Park to hot fudge sundaes. And to you, dear reader, my sincere thanks for spending time with each of the small snippets enclosed.

About the Author

Kristen Zory King is a writer based in Washington, DC. Recent work can be found in *Electric Lit*, *The Citron Review*, *Emerge Literary Journal*, and *Stanchion Zine*, among other publications. In addition to her work on the page, Kris is also a creative teaching artist and yoga instructor. She is currently at work on a project exploring vocation, wonder, and the human spirit. Learn more, join a workshop, or be in touch at www.KristenZoryKing.com.

About the Author

Kristen Zory King is a writer based in Washington, DC. Recent work can be found in *Flowers & Tp*, *The Citron Review*, *Emerge Literary Journal*, and *Sunshine Zine*, among other publications. In addition to her work on the page, KzK is also a creative teaching artist and yoga instructor. She is currently at work on a project exploring vocation, wonder, and the human spirit. Learn more, join a workshop, or be in touch at www.KristenZoryKing.com.